Little Star

FAIRY SCHOOL

Little Star

by Gail Herman

illustrated by Fran Gianfriddo

A Skylark Book

New York • Toronto • London • Sydney • Auckland

RL 2.5, AGES 006–009

LITTLE STAR

A Bantam Skylark Book / March 2000

ISBN: 0-553-48708-6

Visit us on the Web! www.randomhouse.com/kids
Educators and librarians, for a variety of teaching tools, visit us at
www.randomhouse.com/teachers

Published simultaneously in the United States and Canada

Bantam Skylark is an imprint of Random House Children's Books, a division of
Random House, Inc. SKYLARK BOOK, BANTAM BOOKS, and the rooster
colophon are registered trademarks of Random House, Inc. Bantam Books, 1540
Broadway, New York, New York 10036.

PRINTED IN THE UNITED STATES OF AMERICA

CWO 10 9 8 7 6 5 4 3 2 1

For Sam,
our first little star

Little Star

Chapter 1

Bright and early Monday morning, Olivia Skye flew to Fairy School with her three best friends: Trina Larkspur, Dorrie Windmist, and Belinda Dentalette.

The fairies—all three inchworms high—landed on the first-grade branch of their school-tree, then settled by their toadstool-desks. Immediately Belinda hopped back up.

"What do you think we'll do in school today?" she asked excitedly. "I hope there's lots of fairy-flipping and rainbow sliding."

Dorrie sighed. "We did tons of that last week." She rubbed her left wing and made a funny face. "My wing still hurts from when I fell off Cloud Nine and bumped the Fairy Godmother Statue."

Olivia smiled. Leave it to Belinda to want to zip around and Dorrie to make a joke out of being clumsy. "I hope we carve snow-flakes," she told her friends. "We're doing a lot of painting in my other art class, and I could use the practice."

Olivia was such a talented artist that she was in a special art class with taller fairy students. She loved to spend hours tucked away in the peaceful crook of a tree, painting flowers, drawing designs on butterfly wings, or sculpting cloud models. She liked quiet fairy work—school assignments that she could do alone.

Trina stacked her books, then glanced up as the teacher flew onto the branch. "Well, Ms. Periwinkle is here," she said sensibly. "So we'll find out soon enough!"

"Good morning." The teacher fluttered past her barkboard and nodded to the class. "I have a special announcement to make."

Olivia sat up straight. When Ms. Periwinkle said she had an announcement, it was always something exciting. Once, she had announced a big cloud contest to shape the lead cloud in the Fairy Cloud Parade, and another time it was a visit from the Sugar-Plum Fairy.

"Our class is going to put on a play!"

A show! The fairy class clapped and giggled until Ms. Periwinkle clapped her wings for quiet.

"Well, class, what play shall we put on?"

Olivia waved her wing tip to get Ms. Periwinkle's attention. She knew the perfect story. It was her favorite fairy tale of all—the one about Tinkerbell. She thought it had everything. Friendship between the fairy Tinkerbell and the Little Big Person called Peter Pan. Exciting chases with the evil pirate Captain Hook. An enchanted place called Never-Never-Land, where a group called the Lost Boys lived, and Little Big People named Wendy, John, and Michael Darling came to visit. There was even a silly crocodile that swallowed a clock and went *tick, tick, tick.*

Olivia was eager to say *Tinkerbell.* But then she worried: What if Ms. Periwinkle thought she'd made the suggestion because she wanted a role in the play? She certainly didn't want to go onstage in front of the whole school!

I just won't say a thing, Olivia decided, and pulled her wing back down.

Trina, sitting next to her, whispered, "What's going on?"

"I thought I'd suggest the story of Tinkerbell, but then I changed my mind."

"Why?"

Olivia didn't answer. She only shook her head.

"I know why," Trina said softly. "You're feeling too shy!"

"How about the story of Snow White?" a fairy named Sebastian offered. "There are lots of fairies in that one! Remember when Snow White is first born, and they all give her special gifts?"

"Hey! I can play the queen of the fairies," put in Laurel, another fairy student. She lowered her voice, trying to sound modest.

"I am quite a good actress—at least that's what people tell me."

Dorrie snorted. "Sure, you're a good actress—when you're trying to pass the blame for a nasty trick onto another fairy."

Laurel was always doing something mean, like spying or cheating or making up stories just to get her way.

"Excuse me?" Laurel said innocently to Dorrie. "Did you say something?"

"I said—"

"Now, class," Ms. Periwinkle interrupted gently. "We're getting off the subject. Are there any other plays you'd like?"

"There's the Fairy Godmother story," another student said. "You know, the one with the Big Person called Cinderella."

"I can play the Fairy Godmother!" Laurel announced. "As everyone knows, I'm great at turning pumpkins into coaches!"

"Anything else?" Ms. Periwinkle asked.

"Well, whatever it is, I'll be perfect for the lead," Laurel said smugly.

Trina nudged Olivia. But Olivia was still keeping quiet. "All right, I'll do it myself," Trina said. Sighing, she raised her wing. "How about *Tinkerbell*?"

"Terrific idea!" said Sebastian.

Belinda fluttered in circles. "I love it!"

"Me too!" Dorrie exclaimed. "There's no better fairy story than *Tinkerbell*!"

"*Tinkerbell* it is!" Ms. Periwinkle declared.

She waved her magic wand. All at once, a stack of scripts appeared on her desk. She tapped the papers. The scripts floated out to the students, and each fairy took one.

"Read all the parts carefully," Ms. Periwinkle instructed. "We'll have auditions on Friday!"

Chapter 2

The rest of Olivia's day was filled with tooth fairy lessons and wish-granting class and snowflake carving, but she couldn't concentrate. She was too busy thinking about *Tinkerbell*. Her friends were excited too. When school finally ended, they decided to fly straight to Fairyland Meadow and talk more about the play.

"I'll meet you later," Olivia told them in her quiet way, already flying off the branch. "Right now, I have to hurry home to fairy-sit."

***

"Look at us, Wivvy!"

"Watch this!"

Two laughing voices floated down to Olivia as she neared the Skye family tree-house. Quickly she gazed up at the clouds.

"Oh, no!" she cried. "Nicholas! Natalia! Be careful!"

Olivia's brother and sister—chubby, blue-eyed toddler twins—were about to somer-sault off the very top leaf of their family tree-house. Olivia didn't know if their little wings could flap fast enough to keep them from falling.

They tumbled into the air, dropping faster and faster. Olivia flew up to catch them. But they slipped right past her open arms.

Olivia squeezed her eyes shut, afraid to look. When she opened them a second later, Nicholas and Natalia were floating by her side, smiling happily.

"See?" Nicholas said. He patted Olivia's cheek. "Natty and me are good flyers!"

Natalia kissed Olivia's nose. Then she grinned at Nicholas. "More tumbles?"

Before Nicholas could answer, Olivia pulled them safely to the ground. "Now listen, you two," she said, trying to sound firm. "No more crazy flying tricks."

"Crazy flying tricks?" Nicholas said innocently.

"Us?" added Natalia.

Olivia laughed. The twins were always

flipping and slipping and could never sit still for more than a few seconds. But Olivia loved to fairy-sit for them.

She brushed Natalia's blond curls away from her forehead, then gave Nicholas a quick hug. She had to come up with something to keep them busy right here in their own backyard. What would be so exciting that they'd want to keep their feet on the ground?

"Hey!" Olivia said suddenly. "Let's act out *Tinkerbell*!"

Olivia had told the twins the Tinkerbell story so many times, they knew exactly what she meant.

"Okay!" Natalia's face lit up.

"Fun!" Nicholas laughed.

Olivia rubbed her wings. "I'll be Tinkerbell. Nicholas, you be Peter. And

Natalia, you be the Little Big Girl, Wendy. We'll do the part where Tinkerbell and Peter go to Earth-Below to search for his lost shadow, and they meet Wendy."

Olivia fluttered her wings and rose off the ground, pretending to be Tinkerbell.

"Peter!" she cried to Nicholas. "Your shadow is in this closet!"

She and the twins jumped and flew around the backyard, chasing the imaginary shadow.

"Great show!" Olivia heard someone say behind them. She whirled around. Trina was standing nearby, clapping.

"Hi, Trina," Olivia said quietly. She and Trina had known each other since they were one inchworm high, and they were as close as sisters. But still, she'd had no idea anyone was watching. She felt embarrassed.

"I didn't know you could act like that," Trina said.

"That's not acting." Olivia ducked her head. "That's just playing around with the twins."

She could never ever act—not in front of other fairies, not in a million sunsets!

Chapter 3

Trina had come to see if Olivia was finished fairy-sitting. When Mr. and Mrs. Skye came home, the two friends hurried to meet Belinda and Dorrie at Fairyland Meadow, carrying picnic snacks in their fairypacks.

"Hi, you two!" Belinda was perched at the top of the waterfall slide. "We're still talking about *Tinkerbell*. There are so many great roles!" she continued. "Peter, the Lost Boys, Captain Hook. I can't decide which one I want to try out for!" She zoomed down the slide, landing softly on a bed of moss. "What about you, Dorrie?"

Dorrie was under the bright yellow sun shower, drying off from the slide. "I'm not sure," she said. She shook out her long, unruly curls, then grinned. "But I'm thinking about Tinkerbell—just so Laurel won't be the only fairy trying to get the part."

"No one is trying out for Tinkerbell, because everyone thinks Laurel will definitely get it," Trina said, shaking her head. She parted the long, drooping branches of the weeping willow tree and waved a wing at Dorrie and Belinda. Olivia was already setting out fairy-berry snacks and honey-sticks in the tree's cool shade.

"Boo-hoo!" the weeping willow tree

sobbed. "That Laurel is so mean! She doesn't deserve to be the star of anything!"

Trina dabbed at the tree's giant tears with a napkin. Then she glanced at Olivia. "You've been quiet," she told her friend.

"I've been thinking," Olivia said softly. She loved the play so much! And she would love to play Tinkerbell. But she couldn't go onstage. Could she? "I guess I'll just paint scenery for the show. I'd be much too embarrassed to act in front of an audience."

Trina shook her head sadly. "But you were so wonderful just now, acting out the story with the twins. You *were* Tinkerbell!"

Belinda scooted under Mr. Willow. "Olivia as Tinkerbell? That would be fantastic!"

"You'd be great, Olivia," Dorrie pleaded, tumbling under the tree. "I've seen you play-acting with Nicholas and Natalia too."

"You have?" Olivia blushed.

Dorrie nodded. "And you can really act!"

Mr. Willow stopped weeping. Olivia looked at him, surprised. "Oh," he said, "just thinking about you in that role makes me so happy, I can't cry!"

"I'm sorry." Olivia bowed her head, and her blond hair fell over her eyes. "I don't think I can do it."

Belinda twirled in a circle. "Of course you can!"

"That's right," Dorrie added. "We believe in you, Olivia. Even if you don't believe in yourself."

Trina flew close to Olivia and put one wing around her shoulders. "Why don't you audition, at least? It's not like being in the real play, and then you can see how comfortable you feel acting out the role."

Mr. Willow shook his branches excitedly. "Of course, of course! Just audition. And then see what happens."

Olivia looked from Trina to Belinda to Dorrie. Everyone thought she could do it. And it was true: She loved pretending to be Tinkerbell. But still . . .

"Please!" her friends begged, all speaking at the same time.

"We're not giving up until you say yes," Dorrie declared.

Finally Olivia grinned. "I'll do it!"

Chapter 4

All that week, Olivia carried the *Tinkerbell* script everywhere. She wanted to memorize all Tinkerbell's lines—and everyone else's too.

"Olivia!" Mr. Skye exclaimed when he accidentally stirred page seventeen into the batter for Pixie Pancakes. "Please keep those pages together."

"I'm sorry, Dad."

"That's okay, hon. I know you want to do a good job for the audition."

"We're so proud of you for trying," Mrs. Skye added.

"Wivvy's going to be a star!" Nicholas said.

"A real live star!" Natalia crowed.

Night after night, Olivia read and reread the script by the light of the firefly lamp in her room.

And then it was Friday, and time for the auditions.

✳✳✳

The first-grade branch bustled with fairy students flitting here and there, practicing lines.

Olivia stood with her friends. She peered around anxiously.

"You'll do just fine," Trina said, patting her wing. "Just try to relax."

"I know what you can do," Dorrie suggested. "Pretend you're playing with Nicholas and Natalia and no one else is here."

Olivia brightened. "Do you think that would work?"

Belinda nodded. "It's worth a try."

"All right, class!" Ms. Periwinkle hovered above the branch, trying to get everyone's attention. "Those of you who'd like to try out for Peter, please fly to the cloud on your left. Those of you not sure which role you want, go to the right."

Then Ms. Periwinkle pointed to the school meadow. "Fairies interested in playing Tinkerbell, please wait below. When your turn is over, please stay quietly on our class branch."

The students scattered, and soon Olivia found herself standing in the school meadow—alone with Laurel.

Laurel took out a seashell mirror and began to primp, fixing her hair, opening her eyes wide, then blinking them fast, making kissing faces at her reflection.

"Who else can sparkle as brightly?" she asked herself. "Who else is as talented?"

"No one!" the mirror answered.

Laurel grinned. "See?" she taunted Olivia. "I don't know why you're even trying out, when you'd be happier painting quietly in some corner. I'm going to get this part, as surely as the sun rises."

"That's the truth!" the mirror exclaimed.

Olivia knew the talking mirror was just a silly fairy trick to make her nervous. But it was working!

Laurel snapped the mirror shut, then

sneered at Dorrie, "As for you, Miss Olivia Skye! You barely speak above a whisper. How can you possibly play Tinkerbell? No one will hear a word you say."

Olivia blushed and took a step back. "Do you really think that's true?" she asked.

"What's that?" Laurel put a wing to her ear. "You have to speak up, Olivia!"

Olivia winced. Then she saw Ms. Periwinkle flying closer. The teacher would know what she should do.

"It's just the two of you?" the teacher asked Olivia and Laurel, flipping through some papers on a clipboard.

"Ms. Periwinkle," Olivia began. "I have a question."

At that very moment, Laurel sneezed loudly. Ms. Periwinkle kept turning pages, not realizing Olivia had spoken. She didn't hear me! Olivia realized. Maybe I *am* too quiet.

"All right, Laurel," Ms. Periwinkle said. "Why don't you go first?"

"Ahem!" Laurel cleared her throat. She wiggled her wings importantly, patted her hair, and smoothed her dress. "Oh, Peter! Your shadow is in this closet!" she recited in a loud voice.

Olivia opened her eyes wide. Laurel would be heard in the very last row, that was for sure. She sighed, listening as Laurel's voice grew louder and louder. There's no way I'm going to get this part! she thought.

A few lines later, Laurel took a bow. "No way you can be louder than me," she gleefully whispered to Olivia before she flew off to join her class.

Ms. Periwinkle smiled at Olivia. "Your

turn!" She checked the sun and noted the time. "Please begin. We have to move along quickly!"

Olivia took a deep breath. There was no more time to worry. She had to give her Tinkerbell speech. Now!

Chapter 5

"Oh, Peter," Olivia began. "Your shadow is in this closet. . . ."

As she recited a few more lines, the school meadow and Ms. Periwinkle seemed to disappear. Olivia felt as if she really were in a house on Earth-Below, discovering Peter Pan's shadow.

Then she paced in a small square, as if she

were stuck in a dresser drawer in Wendy's room. "Peter!" she called. "I'm in here! I'm trying to get out!"

She pushed harder and harder, and then tumbled to the ground, as if the drawer had sprung open. Olivia jumped up quickly. "I'm free!" she declared. She bent her legs, ready for flight, then took off.

"Not so fast, young fairy," Ms. Periwinkle called out.

"Huh?" Olivia froze, confused. The meadow and Ms. Periwinkle came back into focus. Olivia shook her head. That's right, she remembered. I've been acting out a scene from *Tinkerbell*! But how did I do? She had no idea.

"We can fly to the class branch together," Ms. Periwinkle said with a smile.

✳✳✳

Trailing behind Ms. Periwinkle, Olivia flew to the first-grade branch. Her friends were already sitting at their toadstool-desks.

"How did it go?" Dorrie asked excitedly.

"Not very well," Olivia said slowly. "Laurel was much louder than I was. I don't even know if Ms. Periwinkle heard my speech!"

"Don't give up hope yet." Trina gave her a quick hug.

Ms. Periwinkle waved her clipboard, and the class quieted down. "All right, everyone. I'm going to announce the cast." She gazed from student to student, then stopped at Dorrie. "Dorrie will be playing Captain Hook."

"Hooray!" Dorrie shouted loudly, then clapped a wing over her mouth.

"Belinda will be Peter Pan."

"Hooray!" Dorrie shouted again.

The Lost Boys will be played by Trina, Sebastian, and Lucas."

Trina beamed. She loved the part where the Lost Boys listened to Tinkerbell's stories.

"But what about Tinkerbell?" Laurel asked sweetly. "Of course, we all know what a great Tinkerbell I'll be," she added quickly.

"Well," Ms. Periwinkle continued. "Tinkerbell is . . ."

The class fell silent, listening.

"Olivia Skye!"

"What?" Laurel and Olivia gasped at the same time.

"But Laurel's right. I'm too quiet!" Olivia whispered to her friends. "I'll never be able to do it! I'm going to tell Ms. Periwinkle I can't play the role."

"Come on!" said Trina. "We all have parts. We'll be with you the whole time!"

"That's right," Dorrie agreed. She chuckled like the evil Captain Hook and twirled an imaginary mustache. "And if you don't take this part, I'll make you walk the plank!"

Belinda laughed. "Do it! And I'll be your best friend—in real life *and* because I'm Peter Pan!"

Olivia smiled. "Well . . ."

"Quiet, everyone!" Laurel commanded. "Olivia Skye—mousy little Olivia Skye—can't play Tinkerbell! Ms. Periwinkle, that part should be mine!"

Ms. Periwinkle shook her head. "You're being rude, Laurel. My mind is made up. You can, however, be the understudy. If anything happens so that Olivia can't play the part, you'll be Tinkerbell."

"That's not good enough!" Laurel said, pouting.

"And you'll have an important role as well," Ms. Periwinkle told her. "You'll be the crocodile!"

Chapter 6

The school bell chimed, and the fairies rose from their seats.

"Now you *have* to take the part," Belinda whispered to Olivia, "or that awful Laurel will be the star! And we'll never hear the end of it."

Olivia giggled softly.

"So what do you say?" Trina slung her

fairypack over her shoulder and flew closer, with Dorrie right behind.

"Will you play Tinkerbell?" Dorrie asked.

Olivia still felt nervous. And she still felt that maybe—just maybe—Laurel was right. Maybe she was too quiet to play the lead. But when it came right down to it, Olivia really did want to be Tinkerbell.

"Yes!"

"Great!" Belinda bounced up and down. "Let's go to Fairyland Meadow and celebrate."

"We can tell the Babbling Brook the news, and you know how that stream likes to gossip. Pretty soon he'll be babbling the news to everyone in Fairyland!"

"I'd like to go home first," Olivia told her friends. "And let my parents and Nicholas and Natalia know."

"Sure," Trina agreed. "Today is Friday, so

we have the whole weekend to celebrate—
and rehearse."

Olivia nodded seriously. She thought about
Laurel. "I definitely need the practice."

***

"Congratulations, Olivia!" Mr. Skye hugged
her tight.

"You're going to be terrific!" Mrs. Skye
announced.

Olivia grinned. "I hope so."

Bang! Boom! Nicholas and Natalia
charged into the tree-house at full speed.
"What?" cried Natalia. "Wivvy—play
Tinkerbell?"

"Us help!" Nicholas shouted. He paused a
moment, then added, "How?"

Olivia reached down to hold them both
tight. "I'll show you," she said. "Come out-
side right now!"

Olivia led Nicholas and Natalia to a shady spot in the yard. "Remember how we put on the play the other day? Well, we can do it again."

All afternoon Olivia rehearsed with the twins. Sometimes they had roles and sometimes they were the audience, making sure Olivia was loud enough to be heard.

Early the next morning, Trina flew over. Olivia looked at her fairypack, stuffed to the brim with books and lily notepads and jars of different colored liquids. "That fairypack looks as if it belongs to Dorrie," she joked. "It's so filled with odds and ends."

"Don't laugh," Trina told her. "These odds and ends are going to help you perform."

She emptied the fairypack on the ground. Everything tumbled into neat piles—notepads here, books there, and the jars

lined up in a row. Then she reached back in for a giant clamshell.

Trina waved at the books. "I've been doing lots of research to find magic recipes that will make your voice louder."

"Well?" Olivia asked. "Did you find any?"

"One." Trina flipped through a large, heavy book and stopped at a page near the middle. Olivia gazed over her shoulder at the words: SHOUTS AND ROARS.

"I'm not sure exactly what it will do," Trina admitted. "But we can try."

She put a dash from each jar into the clamshell. "One spoonful of nectar, one pinch of ground leaf, plus a big dollop of tree sap."

Olivia made a face as Trina stirred the dark mixture. "That is going to taste awful."

"Now, one last ingredient. A sprinkle of fresh rainwater."

Olivia added the raindrops. Then she sat back and smiled. "There!"

She poured everything into a walnut-shell cup. "Drink up, Olivia."

Olivia sniffed the cup. "I'm not sure I want to."

"Come on," Trina urged.

Olivia held her nose, lifted the cup to her mouth, and swallowed. Her face turned bright red. She coughed. At last she looked at Trina and smiled.

"That wasn't so bad," she said in a louder voice. "Hey! The recipe worked. My voice *is getting even louder. Thanks . . ." ROAR!*

A thundering lion's roar came out of her mouth!

"Oops!" said Olivia. "How did that—"
CAW CAW!

She sounded like a crow shouting noisily.

"What's going—"

43

AWHOO!

Now she sounded like a wolf howling at the moon.

Olivia clapped a wing over her mouth, determined not to say anything else.

Trina paced back and forth. "Well, that didn't work. I'd better reverse everything."

She waved her magic wand and said: *"Olivia's voice come back to stay. No animal noises can be in the play."*

"Thank you, Trina," Olivia said in her own soft way.

"Maybe we should make up a different spell," Trina said, waving her wand.

"I don't know about that." Dorrie thudded to a landing in the backyard, and Belinda settled gracefully beside her.

"I don't think magic potions or spells are

the way to go," Dorrie continued. "What if they wear off in the middle of the performance? You might not be able to mix another potion or recite another rhyme."

Olivia sighed. "That's right. Maybe my own voice is best after all."

"Of course it is!" Belinda exclaimed. Dorrie nodded, and Trina agreed.

"No one's better at talking loudly than me," Dorrie told Olivia. "You know, I have to concentrate on keeping my voice *down*."

"That's true," Trina said. "Just think how many times the spider librarian hushes Dorrie when we go to the library!"

Dorrie giggled. Then she turned serious and said to Olivia, "Listen. Just try talking from deep in your stomach. Hold your head high and talk to . . ." She peered across the yard. "That daisy over there."

The daisy waved a leaf. "I hear you loud and clear, Dorrie."

"My turn," Olivia said, standing as tall as she could. "Hello, Daisy!"

The daisy held a leaf up to its petals. "What's that?"

"Hello, Daisy!"

"Wait," said Dorrie. "Don't shout. Just speak forcefully."

"Hello, Daisy."

"Why, hello, Olivia!"

"I did it!" Olivia cried. Then she shook her head. "But I'm still nervous about acting in front of an audience."

Belinda stepped close to Olivia. "You just have to move those nervous tummy flutters up to your wings, and use them to fly! Like this." She flapped her wings three more times, then jumped up and down. "That shakes the flutters loose," she explained.

Olivia fluttered and jumped exactly like Belinda. "I think it's working," she said. She smiled broadly at her friends, one after the other. "But there's one thing I know for sure. I definitely feel better about playing Tinkerbell—thanks to all of you!"

Chapter 7

By the time Olivia went to school Monday morning, she felt more ready to perform than ever. She stood by her desk to recite the Fairy School Pledge and spoke in a loud, firm voice.

A few desks over, Laurel snorted. "If that's your stage voice," she told Olivia, "you'd better tell everyone in the audience to sit in the first row. Otherwise no one will hear."

"Don't listen to her." Trina patted Olivia's shoulder.

Olivia jumped up and down until she felt the flutters in her stomach rise to her wings. "You know what?" she said to Trina. "I am going to be Tinkerbell!" Suddenly she felt one more teeny-tiny flutter in her tummy. "I just hope nothing goes wrong."

"Hmm." Laurel sat at her desk and pretended she didn't hear the friends talking. "But what if something *does* go wrong?"

✳✳✳

A little while later, the first-grade class assembled on the rock-stage in the meadow for rehearsal.

"Now, you haven't had much time to memorize your lines," Ms. Periwinkle told

49

the actors. "So hold your scripts while we go through the play." She clapped her wings. "Let's start from the beginning. Tinkerbell! Peter Pan! You're on!"

Olivia stepped onto the stage with Belinda, who grinned.

"Let's do it!" Belinda whispered.

Olivia nodded slowly as she gazed at her classmates, who were staring back at her. She seemed to be doing everything slowly, as if she were swimming through honey. There were so many fairies watching! And this was just the first grade, not the whole school.

Olivia clutched her script. Of course she knew her lines by heart—and everyone else's too! But what if she suddenly forgot them? What if she couldn't remember a thing?

Thank goodness Ms. Periwinkle had said they could keep their pages.

"Oh, Tink," Belinda began to recite. "Where could my shadow be? Do you think . . . do you think maybe it's here, on Earth-Below?"

Olivia didn't answer.

"Tink?" Belinda repeated, giving Olivia a nudge. "I said, 'Where could my shadow be?'"

Olivia couldn't remember what to say. "What's that line?" she asked herself. She riffled through her script. Suddenly the pages slipped out of her hands. Each page turned into a pretty white dove and flew quickly away.

Everyone laughed and clapped at the trick. But Ms. Periwinkle shook her head. "If you need help, Olivia, just ask for it," she said sternly. "Putting on a play is serious work."

Olivia turned bright red. "I'm s-s-sorry,"

she stammered. "I don't know what could have happened!"

A little distance away, Laurel hid her magic wand behind her wings and smiled.

Chapter 8

How did that happen? Olivia wondered. She'd felt embarrassed when her script pages flew away, and a little confused too. But then she fluttered and jumped and felt calm.

"All right, Ms. Periwinkle," she called. "I'm ready to try again."

Ms. Periwinkle nodded. Olivia smiled at

Belinda. "I'll start with my first line," she told her friend. She paused a moment, taking a deep breath. "Peter, I think I know where your shadow might be . . ."

Belinda spoke next, then Olivia. Little by little, Olivia forgot about the other first-graders watching and the script in her hand. The only thing she thought was: I am Tinkerbell.

Then, right in the middle of an important scene, she heard a soft whooshing noise coming from above. She looked up just as the leaf curtain fell on her head.

The class erupted in laughter once more. Olivia's speech was ruined. "Okay, everyone!" Ms. Periwinkle announced. "We may as well stop right now. But we'll rehearse every day this week. The big performance will be on Friday!"

Flying home with Trina, Olivia shrugged

her wings and tried to make herself feel better. "So my script turned into doves and the curtain fell on my head. That's not such a big deal."

Trina looked at her admiringly. "Good for you!" she said.

But why did those things happen? Olivia couldn't help wondering. Could it have been Laurel? Up to her old nasty tricks? She couldn't say for sure.

The next day during rehearsal, mosquitoes buzzed so loudly during one of Olivia's speeches that she had to stop talking.

"Okay," she told herself. "You can get through this too."

On Wednesday the class concentrated on one of the quieter scenes: Tinkerbell telling stories to the Lost Boys. "Once upon a time . . . ," Olivia began.

Suddenly the firefly stage lights darted

around, shining right in her eyes. Blinded and startled, Olivia lost her balance. She felt herself falling. She landed—*splash!*—in the ocean, which was supposed to be used in the big scene with Captain Hook and had mysteriously appeared below.

So many disasters!

Yet somehow, with everything that was going wrong, Olivia was hanging in there, doing her best. And her best was very good. Strangely enough, all the disasters were making her feel more confident!

"I'm going to be the best Tinkerbell ever," she told Trina the day before the show.

"Not if I can help it!" Laurel muttered, hiding behind Peter's shadow, which was hanging on a tree branch.

Chapter 9

The hours flew by, and the next thing Olivia knew, it was almost show time. Backstage, everyone was bustling around, getting ready. Olivia peeked at the audience from behind the curtain of leaves. She saw students, friends, families—and her parents sitting in the first row with Nicholas and Natalia on their laps.

"Look!" cried Natalia, spying Olivia. "It's Wivvy!"

"Let's go!" Nicholas shouted.

A second later, they were fluttering around backstage. "Natty and Nicky stay?" Natalia asked Olivia. "Please?"

"Watch from here! Pretty please!" Nicholas begged.

Olivia didn't have time to argue with the twins. That could take hours! Sighing, she nodded. "But wait here quietly. Don't move. I have to get my costume on, and then I'll be right back!"

She hurried to the dressing space. For a few minutes, Nicholas and Natalia stayed still. Everyone was in such a hurry, no one noticed the tiny toddlers—and no one noticed Laurel, off in a far corner, bent over a pile of twigs. No one but the twins.

"What Laurel doing?" Nicholas asked.

Natalia shrugged. "Go look?" she asked.

Nicholas nodded, and they took off, circling quietly over Laurel's head.

"Laurel make big hole," Nicholas whispered.

"Now Laurel making door," Natalia said softly.

"This is going to be great," Laurel muttered to herself. She was weaving a door with a lock and a hinge out of twigs and fitting it on the ground next to a large hole.

"I'll call Olivia, then hide. She'll fall into the hole. The door will flip over the hole, the lock will snap shut, and she'll be trapped! Then I'll play Tinkerbell!" Laurel chuckled.

"Laurel telling joke!" Natalia said, not understanding. "Ha, ha!"

Nicholas joined in, laughing loudly.

Laurel jumped in surprise and teetered on the edge of the hole.

"Oops!" she shouted, and fell right into the trap. *Click!* The door locked above her. "Let me out!" she called to Nicholas and Natalia.

"Oops!" said Nicholas.

"Better get back to Mama," Natalia said, and off they scampered.

"Help!" Laurel cried. And then she clapped a wing over her mouth. She shouldn't be shouting for help. She didn't want everyone to see the trap and realize she'd been trying to trick Olivia.

"How am I ever going to get out?" she moaned.

Chapter 10

A few minutes later, Olivia—wearing her soft, filmy costume and her makeup—was searching for the twins.

"Oh, I shouldn't have left them alone. Not even for a minute," she scolded herself. "Now I have to find them before the show starts."

She wandered farther and farther from the center of activity, winding up in a distant corner. Suddenly she tripped on a pile of twigs. No, she realized, it wasn't really a pile. It was more like a . . . like a door!

Then she heard muffled crying.

"Hello?" she called. "Is someone under there?"

"It's me," Laurel said, sniffling.

"Laurel! What are you doing down there?"

"I'm trapped!" Laurel answered.

"Don't worry. I'll get you out." Olivia pulled at the door. It was heavier than it looked. She gave a big tug, and the door swung open.

"There!" Olivia said as Laurel flew out to join her.

Laurel sighed and sat heavily on the ground. "Thanks for helping me," she said quietly. "I'm not sure I deserve it."

"Why not?" asked Olivia.

Laurel was silent for a second. Then she told Olivia everything—about her secret spells and all her mean tricks. "Maybe this last trick was *too* mean," Laurel said. "Anyway, I'm sorry for everything I did to you. It's just that I wanted to play Tinkerbell so much!"

"I understand," Olivia said. And she did—because she wanted to play Tinkerbell too.

Just then the school chimes sounded. The show was about to begin.

Laurel jumped up. "Well, I'd better get into my crocodile costume! You're going to be great, Olivia."

***

For Olivia, the play went by in a blur. One minute she was saying her first line, the next minute she was taking a bow.

65

And then the fairies in the audience were on their feet, clapping their wings so hard that they sounded like thunder. The show was a hit. And Olivia knew she was a hit too. She'd been so nervous—afraid she'd speak too quietly, anxious about acting in front of a crowd—but she'd come through, and she was glad!

Olivia hugged Trina, then Belinda and Dorrie. She couldn't have done it without her three best friends. Then she walked to the front of the rock-stage to take a bow, all alone.

The audience flew to their feet. Smiling, Olivia beckoned to the rest of the cast to come forward. She stood with Trina, Belinda, and Dorrie and nodded happily at all her classmates—except Laurel. Laurel wasn't there!

Olivia wheeled around. Laurel was huddling at the corner of the stage, behind a curtain. Why, she still feels bad about her tricks! Olivia thought.

She flew over and gently pulled Laurel forward.

The applause grew even louder, and Olivia grinned at Laurel.

"See?" she whispered. "We're all stars!"

The Fairy School Pledge

(sung to the tune of "Twinkle, Twinkle, Little Star")

We are fairies
Brave and bright.
Shine by day,
Twinkle by night.

We're friends of birds
And kind to bees.
We love flowers
And the trees.

We are fairies
Brave and bright.
Shine by day,
Twinkle by night.